Julia Emote

LET`S TALK
ABOUT
BODY BOUNDARIES

gardening club

THIS BOOK BELONGS TO

Meet Chloe! She is a young lady who loves
her long plaits, her parents, and her school gardening club!
She grows fruit trees and takes care of rare flowers.

Charlie is often not aware of his own strength, so he plays way too rough during games.

— You'll be it! — he exclaimed, trying to tag Chloe. Not feeling like up for this game, Chloe quickly gathered her school bag and headed home.

— GUESS what? Your Granny from Toronto is coming to visit! — Dad said happily when she got home.
But the news upset Chloe even more.
She wanted to go straight to her room.

— Honey, you seem down. Is everything ok?
— Dad always notices Chloe's mood. Chloe always shares her true feelings with Mom and Dad.

— Daddy, I don't like the way Charlie pulls my pigtails and hugs me too tight,— said Chloe. — And Granny's kisses are sometimes too much, as well as when Lucky jumps on me to show his love.

Dad nodded. — It's okay to feel that way, Chloe. Everyone has their own comfort space.

It's important to tell people, whether it's Charlie or even Granny, when their actions make us uncomfortable. It helps them learn to respect our personal space.

Strangers, friends, even people you are close to, like your Granny – none of them can use your space if you don't want them to. Your body is yours. So, you can choose to simply say "no" and wave or blow a kiss – just let them know your personal boundaries. And Granny will still love you lots, trust me!

Understanding boundaries is easy: imagine someone not just being next to you, but too close – so close that you would like to turn or even walk away. This is your personal space, your own invisible bubble, and you decide who to let inside.

— Dad, do my thoughts and feelings also have boundaries? Yesterday Lucy said we couldn't be friends if I don't join the swimming club with her. But I want to learn rollerblading! They are so fast and graceful!

— Absolutely! To live a happy and full life, we all need to make our own choices and express our own thoughts and emotions.

— You can show your love and respect by giving personal space to those you care about. That means you can be much closer in thoughts and feelings, even without your bodies being close to each other.

For example, when mom is doing a workout, you should wait until she finishes, then she will help you with your school homework.

And when I am on a video call - this could be a good time for you to have fun with your stickers or draw a picture of me working.

If you'd like to enter a room where Mom or Dad are, a gentle 'knock-knock' on the door is exactly what a caring person would do.

One of the most private parts of each of us is hidden behind our underwear. We do not show these to others, and trying to see or touch them is rude and dangerous – you should call and run for help straight away if someone does.

— But what about doctor visits? Can he ask me
to show my body to him? — asked Chloe.
— That is a good question! Our bodies might be poorly
or need a check-up, and that is the doctor's job.
Anyway, me or Mommy will always come with you for that.

— What about the strangers? How can I tell when something is wrong?
— Chloe, you are a smart girl and ask clever questions. So, friendly strangers are fine, as long as they are not asking you to go somewhere with them or not giving you sweets to do something for that. If that happens, you should call one of your Palm Crew for help.

— Palm Crew is how you remember the people you trust the most: each of your fingers is a person, and you are the palm of the hand. Let's see. That could be Mom and me, your cousin, Granny and your teacher – that's five people who are always there to help you. But if none of us are around, ask any adult for help or leave as soon as you can.

Chloe was happy she had told Dad her worries and asked all her questions. Now she knows about her personal space and how to protect it, and how to respect the personal space of others.

The next day Chloe went to the swimming pool with Lucy to support her, and Lucy did the same for Chloe afterward — she went to watch Chloe try rollerblades.
— Our friendship is even stronger now!

The next important thing was to meet Charlie at the gardening club.
— I've missed you, friend! Let's plant a berry bush and look after
it together. Chloe was open and told the boy about her boundaries:
she did not like her plaits being pulled.

Charlie was happy they were friends, taking care of each other even
more by respecting each one's personal space. That day Chloe and
Charlie planted a raspberry bush to look after together.

You can make the world a better place for others and for yourself.
But there will always be things you would never want to change...
Like a new bedtime story by Dad and
Mom's goodnight kiss

LET`S TALK WITH CHLOE:

1. What did you learn about keeping your body safe?

2. Can you think of some ways we can show respect for other people's boundaries?

3. Can you imagine a situation when you might need to say "no" to someone?

4. Who are your Palm Crew you would ask for help or have questions about your body?

5. Can you think of something important from this book you would share with your friend when you meet next time?

Braids swinging, boundaries set,
I'm Chloe, don't forget.
Scan this code, a surprise to see,
Let's Talk, please feel free!

My dear little Reader, how are you today?
Thank you for choosing this book to learn about your personal space and body boundaries.
This is the very first book in the "Let's Talk" series about Chloe and her friends.
Join Charles, Lucy, and other friends of Chloe in their discoveries, and, of course, use
this knowledge after in your everyday life.

I have received a lot of positive feedback on "Let's Talk about Body Boundaries" book from
parents and kids. This gives me shivers non-stop and motivates me to continue discovering
the huge world of emotions, feelings, and important skills together with Chloe.

I am grateful to you for being the biggest inspiration for my books, and I will greatly
appreciate you sharing any feedback, thoughts, and ideas, as well as asking questions and
just saying hello to me on juliaemote.com or julia.emote.author@gmail.com
If you enjoyed this book and if you find it giving you the best knowledge,
please write a review of it here:

With love,
Julia Emote

Time to get creative, young artists!
Let's design our own Palm Crew, just like
Chloe's. Grab your colors and turn each
finger into someone special for you –
family, friends, and more.

Put your 5 best people onto your palm
and celebrate the love they bring!
Ready to make your Palm Crew
come to life? Let's go!

Made in United States
North Haven, CT
17 January 2024

47601633R00018